BIG**FAT**

Obsession

Hedonist

Hedonist

CONTENTS

BIG FAT OBSESSION

Darryl:

I stare down at my phone again. At the message from *her*, which I saw the preview of, but left unread.

She wanted to meet up for drinks. The plan has been made weeks ago, when this conference and all the realities of it seemed like a distant, surreal future.

Right now, the cold hard reality of what stands before me seems insurmountable, though. Meeting up for drinks. What a laughable idea. I don't want to meet anyone this weekend. I don't even want to deliver the presentation I've come here to give.

I want to die in a hole, out of sight and far away from everyone who for some strange reason looks to me for answers. People who think I've got it together. That I know what I'm doing. Do I look like I bloody know what I'm doing? My truth isn't just skewed; it's a polar opposite to what everyone expects from me.

From the moment I arrived here, I've found myself in this busy dining hall, with the unlimited buffet, gorging myself on all of it. I barely stopped to breathe in between visits for refills. And every time they pass by with the dessert cart, I've been unable to resist the temptation of just one more pastry. Just one more pudding.

Just one more…

The empty plates piled high on my table are a

testament to my shame. I don't think I could get up right now even if I wanted to. The truth is, I haven't even tried, because it seems easier to stay here, in this time loop, where nothing exists except the frantic racing of my heart and one more dessert.

My breaths are shallow; the edge of the table digs painfully into my belly. My face is clammy and flushed and my hands and knees tremble whenever I do try to move a little.

I'm a willing prisoner on this bench seat, which thankfully has been designed keeping patrons of my size in mind. Or else I would have embarrassed myself even further by crashing right through.

Still, I see the looks I get. I hear the whispers all around. I feel painfully on display, and yet have been completely unable to avoid making a spectacle out of myself. And a lot of these people might know who I am. At least by tomorrow, they'll figure it out. That's the worst part.

This is why I don't leave the house. So I don't have to meet people…

God, I can't face *her*. I didn't think this through at all. She said she's not much into conferences. Large crowds freak her out. But she booked the trip for *me*. To meet *me*. It's too much.

Of all the people I wish to avoid this weekend, most of all, I wish to avoid *her*.

From the very first email she sent me, in response to one of my many podcast episodes, something started to stir in me which I desperately tried to wish away. Except during those moments, just between sleeping and waking, when reality doesn't matter and anything is possible.

During those times, my imagination ran wild. Now that I think back to it, it was during one of those moments that I agreed to meet with her. It felt nice to entertain the idea that maybe it wasn't all just a dream. That maybe those feelings I've felt reading her words, I could experience in person too.

And now, she's reached the conference center and is wondering what time I might be free to put our plan into action. Those drinks, which I never really planned on having. Well, except in my dreams. In a fantasy world, there's a whole lot more I would have been hoping for. But this isn't a fantasy. This is reality.

And in this world, I am not in any condition to meet the woman who has been haunting my thoughts for the better part of four months. No, in this world, I am fit for nothing. I am a disgrace, a failure of a human being, who has somehow tricked a few people into believing that I'm worth listening to.

I've written a few books people like, sure. But those were flukes. And anyway, it's been over a year since I finished any new work. I told myself it was because I was putting more energy into the podcast. That I was helping other authors, just like her.

Incidentally, that's what she wrote about in her first email. She thanked me for all the content I'd been putting out on YouTube and other places. How it had helped her find her voice, and her confidence as a writer. She exaggerated, obviously, because nothing I did was that special.

But it still meant a lot to me. I wrote back immediately, thanking her for the kind words of encouragement, which resulted in a quick back and forth. A daily ritual almost, of emails and DMs, exchanged from afar, isolated from the larger world out there.

Every so often, the messages turned a little suggestive. Just enough to deepen my interest in our exchanges, but never crass or too obvious. That was probably by design, at least from my side. I liked the idea of being able to feign ignorance. To have her be able to back out later and pretend like we weren't flirting with each other. It's safer that way. I never intended for her to get stuck in anything she wasn't ready for. And flirtations with me? Nobody is ready for that.

My phone buzzes again. The screen lights up with a follow up from her.

"Are you okay?"

This. This right here is why I keep coming back to her messages and emails. And why I'm fighting to avoid her so hard right now. Her perceptiveness, which she herself would brush away with self-deprecating humour. She always seems to know exactly what to say to me to hit a nerve.

If she could see me right now, she would look right through me. She would recognise that I'm a charlatan and a fake, and I'd see the disappointment on her face. And then I'd never get another message from her to brighten up a bleak morning. Never another word of encouragement to trick me into thinking I'm on the right track. And then what would life be?

I still haven't opened the messages, though. And I guess she knows it, because I stupidly told her my approximate schedule beforehand. It's obvious that I don't have anywhere else to be right now.

Shit. She knows I'm ignoring her. Hence the follow up. How long will I be able to avoid her, like an absolute coward? Am I going to back out of the presentation and leave here with my tail between my legs? Will I lie about some kind of emergency, requiring me to cut my trip short just to save face?

Or maybe, if I have just a few more of those desserts and god knows what else, an emergency of the self-inflicted kind will present itself, making my excuses for me. I certainly feel ill enough already. It wouldn't be a complete lie.

No, this is quite enough. Just how big a chicken shit am I willing to become? The shame is too much to bear. And with a bit of luck, she will sense what's really going on and not push back on what I'm about to do. I might be able to get through this weekend with at least some of my self-respect intact. She anyway doesn't like crowds. So, if I just hide in plain sight, in the mass of people attending this conference…

It was a nice fantasy, but now it's over.

I take a deep breath, well as deep as I possibly can considering how absolutely stuffed I am right now, and swipe open the notification. Then, I type a quick message to her.

"I don't think it would be right for us to meet. I am sorry."

And then I immediately switch my phone off and toss it aside.

Charlotte:

He doesn't know. He doesn't know the depths I have fallen to. Or maybe he does, and that's why he sent me that devastating message after pretending to ignore me previously.

For the better part of the hour that I've been on site, I've sat here, across the busy dining hall, with the perfect vantage point to watch him. I've observed him visit the buffet half a dozen times; each time carrying back more food than any normal human being should eat in a day, never mind in a single meal. I've seen him stop the dessert tray countless times. And I've watched as he read my message, over and over again, and then put the phone down without ever replying. I also saw the lost expression on his face throughout, even though we're sat quite far apart. It's why I finally sent another message asking if he's okay.

The face he made when he read that nearly ripped my heart out of my chest. He's not okay at all. But exactly what is wrong, I cannot say. I might have made him uncomfortable. Maybe I was too pushy, asking to meet up for drinks. I thought I kept it casual and lighthearted, but then I've always had trouble doing things casually when it comes to matters of the heart.

There's nothing casual about how I feel.

Over the course of the four months we've been in touch, I've fallen deeply. Sure, our messages and emails were mostly innocent. Any innuendo that did crop up could be brushed aside as off-colour humour or misinterpretation. Or so I kept telling myself.

And now that it's almost too real, he's backed out of our plan. Just why, I can't say for sure. My intuition doesn't usually lead me astray, but then again… I have lost perspective when it comes to him.

I'm hopelessly obsessed. Watching him like a stalker, hidden in the crowd.

We've never so much as video chatted, so he only knows me from my avatar; a low resolution headshot from three years ago when my hair was shorter. There's no way he would recognise me from this far off. Whereas I'd know him anywhere, obviously, so I've got him at a disadvantage.

And right now, my imagination is working overtime to figure out what could have gone wrong. I usually assume it's me. Whatever goes wrong in social situations, usually I did something wrong to cause it. I know how I tend to come across. Annoying. Clingy. Desperate. I've heard it all before.

Only this time, I've been so careful. And something tells me all this dilly-dallying and avoiding my messages and especially the binge eating… This wasn't me. This is all him. But why?

And more importantly, how can I help? He's done so much for me, so if there's anything I could do to repay the favour, I'd do it in a heartbeat.

Maybe I should approach him. God. That would be terrifying.

I'm much better in writing than I am in person. But… there's a strange kind of energy coming from his direction. It's pulling me towards him. It's why I sent the second message, after all. And now that it's confirmed that he is not in fact okay…

Also, that apology for not wanting to meet up, that was weird. Somehow it doesn't feel like he's trying to let me down easy. It feels like he's screaming for help, even if the words suggest the opposite.

I *should* approach him. At least I'll get some clarity on whether he really wants me to back off. In person, I'll be able to tell what his intentions are. I'll be able to sense what he *really* needs from me.

Yes, it's the right thing to do. Even if I'm already panicking. My heart is racing and my hands are clammy. But I can no longer ignore the growing urgency rising in my chest. This can't carry on.

I push my chair back and start to walk, one foot in front of the other in resolute steps right across the dining hall, straight to his table.

Turn around! Run! Hide!

I ignore my inner voice, screaming at me to abort the mission, and keep going until I reach him.

"Darryl. Hi."

"Oh fuck," he mutters under his breath.

His eyes, watery and unfocused, linger on mine for just a moment, before looking away again. It hurts to see him like this. There's been an edge to some of his videos in the past, some hidden level of sadness, but it was never overt like it is now.

"Let me start by explaining that I did indeed get your message just now. And it's not my intention to make a scene," I say.

He closes his eyes and tries to catch his breath. He's really struggling with that though. No wonder, considering everything I saw him eat. He's a big man, but still. That was some feat… Some capacity. He must be so uncomfortably full. Why did he do it? This doesn't look fun, no matter how tasty the food might have been or how hungry he was before.

"I really am sorry," he says. His voice sounds rattly and weak. Not at all like how he sounds in his videos. Something is very, very wrong. I hope I wasn't the cause of all this somehow.

"Look, it's okay, really," I lie. Nothing is okay. This weekend was going to be me making my stand. I was going to finally come out with all of it. To be honest and tell him how I really feel, without resorting to subtleties and suggestive jokes that could easily be brushed aside later. And then it was going to be up to him to decide what to do about it.

Sure, I've had my hopes and dreams for this moment, but I always knew that there was a real possibility it would go tits up. But it's already pretty much a disaster, because he tried to cancel on me, so what have I got to lose?

"I can't do this," he mumbles. "I can't–"

He's panting for air almost and leans back a little, but that doesn't really do much. He looks pretty stuck, actually. I wish I could do something to help, but I can't work out what. Why did he eat so damn much? Why didn't he stop sooner?

Because he couldn't. He couldn't stop. There's that inner voice again, making a whole lot of sense this time. Of course he couldn't. It's a compulsion. An addiction. Like me, watching his videos and re-reading his emails, fantasising about things I can't have. I couldn't stop that even if I wanted to.

It's like me, spying on him from across the dining hall for an hour while being completely aware of how shameful that is. Still, there has to be something I could do for him, right?

"Darryl, do you need anything? A glass of water, maybe?" I ask.

He glances up at me, frowning. "Do I look like–" he tries to clear his throat, turning redder in the face as he coughs. "No. Water won't help. But…"

"Yes?"

"I'd like to be alone," he says. Finally, he's able to breathe again, though it's still laboured and rattly.

His request, although reasonable on the surface, goes against everything I sense to be true. No. I couldn't possibly.

"Sure. After I do what I came here to do. Came here to say, rather," I tell him, resting my hand on his shoulder.

He flinches under my touch, and stares at me. The

look in his eyes does not match what's coming out of his mouth either. No, I will not leave him alone in this state. But I'll also not get into an argument right now, so let's both pretend that I'm being agreeable.

"Okay, do tell. What's the point of all of this? Why did you want to meet up?" His tone is still hostile, but his eyes… His eyes are pleading for kindness and mercy.

"Well, the PC version of my purpose here today was to give you a big hug and thank you for everything you've done for me. Through your videos, and all the stuff you've so freely shared, you've actually changed my life. I mean, I know I said as much in various emails before, but… I wanted to do this in person as well. It's more meaningful that way."

He presses his lips together, but I can still see the bottom one trembling ever so slightly. He's not good at taking compliments. That's okay, neither am I.

"Would that be okay?" I ask, stretching my arms out awkwardly in his direction.

I'm not a hugger, either, but well… I do want to hug him, for obvious reasons. Firstly it'll help me figure out how much of what I've been dreaming about is actually real… Secondly, well, it's the best way to express my gratitude in a way that words simply couldn't.

"Knock yourself out," he grumbles.

And so, a deep breath later, I close my eyes and lean across to wrap my arms around his shoulders. His very broad, very fleshy shoulders. It doesn't make a lot of sense, but I try to really feel everything I want to convey to him. All the emotions and sensations and desires and dreams, and pour them into this hug. It's all in the hope that he can feel what I feel, radiating through my hands and arms and the rest of my body, and into him. I snuggle my head against his and inhale his scent, enjoying how it tickles deep in my chest, letting out a content sigh in the process.

"Thank you so much, Darryl. I owe you everything." As I speak, that same tickle in my chest turns into a lump in my throat and the beginnings of tears in the corner of my eyes.

Or maybe it wasn't even just that. It's what I feel from him in return. An intense sadness, which enters and envelops me as his hands tentatively end up on my back. I could stay in his arms forever. If only he'd let me. Maybe I could suck the sadness out of him so that he'd feel lighter again.

He pulls away much too soon and averts his gaze again, though. Still, I notice that his eyes are moist too. Maybe my hug has had some of its desired effect. Maybe I've managed to soften up some of his hostility at the very least.

I sit down next to him on the bench, and for the first time, start observing some of the other people surrounding us. There are some guys in suits, but most people look quite casual, or even quirkily dressed. It's not the usual crowd for a business oriented venue such as this.

"Mostly fellow writers, aren't they?" I say. "Though, I can't say I recognise anyone."

He grunts a reply, but doesn't say anything. Was this

weird for him? He might know people in this crowd. Was it weird that I hugged him in this busy hall, right in front of everyone?

Then again, we might be old friends for all everyone else knows. I've witnessed many exuberant reunions since I've arrived here. I know that many of my more extroverted contemporaries have been looking forward to this conference for months.

I, on the other hand, am much more reserved. The only person I've been dying to meet is sitting right next to me, in silence.

"What's the non-PC version?" he says. "You said that the PC version of your purpose was to thank me."

I hoped he'd pick up on that. And I also hoped that he wouldn't. I press my lips together and try to ignore the goosebumps that have sprouted all over my back and arms, and then I turn part of the way to look at him.

"Well… To tell you the truth."

"Yes?"

"No, that was it. My real purpose was to tell you the truth about… everything, really."

When he glances in my direction, I think I catch him looking me up and down. Like, really looking. Just for a brief moment. It's thrilling. I thought long and hard about what I would wear for our first meeting in the hopes that he would find me attractive. That's what this figure-hugging bodycon dress is all about.

At the very least, I wanted him to notice me in more ways than one. Maybe the hug helped things along that way.

"What truth is that?" he asks.

I swallow my anxiety and fear and really look at him now. No more shy glances, stolen from afar. He's bigger than I thought he'd be, although even in the footage from last year's conference, he was already a big man. If I'm entirely honest with myself, I like it.

I mean, I don't like that he's visibly uncomfortable in his skin. I didn't like watching him stuff himself as much as he did over the past hour. And I certainly don't like seeing him wedged in behind the table, looking stuck and unable to catch a good breath, but…

The truth is, none of what I've found here today has changed a damn thing about how I feel. I have never been more attracted to a man than I am right now.

"It would have been easier to tell you over drinks," I chuckle nervously. "I wouldn't feel quite so put on the spot, you know."

He shakes his head. "I don't, actually."

If this were any other guy, I'd wonder if he's playing games with me. But I can see the confusion written in his face, plain as day.

"Okay, so," I place my hand on top of his, which has been resting on his very thick thigh, then thread my fingers through his. He inhales sharply–loudly–which nearly takes my breath away too. "I'd planned to tell you that all those emails and messages sent back and forth between the two of us… How much it all meant to me."

"U-huh."

Does that mean it meant a lot to him too? I suppose

a clear sign from him would be too much to expect.

"And that over the last four months, I've fallen hopelessly in love with you," I end my confession on a whisper, almost.

His hand pulls away, prompting me to let go.

"You, what?!"

"I mean, I totally understand that this is perhaps unexpected, because I never expressed myself clearly before, but I did get the impression that the little hints and teases I'd been dropping... That you–you know– that you reciprocated..." I mumble.

God, this is a bit of a mess. And I like to pretend that I'm good with words. Well, I guess that's why I'm a writer, because I'm better at writing shit down, rather than saying it out loud.

"Everything between us, it was all just..." He exhales loudly and shrugs. "It was a game, wasn't it? A little bit of fun. Throwing a little bait out there, seeing what would come back. It wasn't *real* in any way, right?"

This was always the risk. I knew it going into this, and I imagined myself going through a very similar conversation every day for weeks leading up to this moment. Still, it's like he hit me right in the gut with a punch hard enough to knock the wind out of me. But much like in my imagined scenarios, I know I have to put it all out there. I have to make it so there is no chance of misinterpreting what's been happening.

"It was always very real to me. Still is," I say, choking back the beginnings of inconvenient emotions. I wasn't going to make a scene I'd said, and I still don't plan to.

Darryl:

"It was always very real to me. Still is," she says.

And I feel like the ground is caving in underneath me. My head is spinning; my heart is beating out of control and I can't quite catch a breath.

This is impossible. This can't be.

"You *cannot* be serious," I hear myself say. "You can't. I can't."

My mind is a dense fog of contradictions. The ones I manage to express are the loudest, revolting against everything she's' telling me. But there's also something else. Something quieter, more hidden, which threatens to bubble to the surface now. The dreams I've had about her; about us. Those which only seem possible when I'm not yet fully awake.

"We were just playing around!" I argue. "Always just subtle enough to be able to deny later."

"We fell into a pattern of communication, sure. But it was never my intention to deny it altogether," she whispers.

Her voice. It's so soft and fragile now. After avoiding looking in her direction throughout her supposed confession, I now see just how small she looks. How wounded and terrified. I can't blame her for that, obviously. But I also fail to understand what the point of telling me this now is. It can no longer be true, because what we shared together, via emails and messages and all the rest of it, it no longer exists. Now we are two very real people out in the real world. Now, there are facts to contend with. And the fact is that this brilliant, sensitive and incredibly perceptive woman has seen my true colours. And so everything she thought she came here to say no longer holds meaning.

"That was then, though. And this is now," I say, almost shocked at how weak my own voice sounds now.

"You don't feel the same," she concludes, leaning back against the bench.

She's so close to me, I can feel the warmth of her leg beside mine. I can catch the flowery scent of her hair. I can almost feel the air vibrate with every one of her breaths.

She's a beautiful woman; gorgeous even. I stole a moment to admire her earlier when she just sat down, and I noted that she's probably the most beautiful woman I've ever seen. By far the most beautiful woman I've ever shared a conversation with. The resemblance to her display picture is there, yes, but I would have never recognised her had she not come up to me. Because instinctively, I would have never really looked at anyone like her. I would have written her off as someone who does not belong in my sphere, because she's otherworldly.

"I mean, I can't really blame you." She shrugs.

What? No! I shake my head.

"Charlotte." It occurs to me that this is the first time I've spoken her name. It tickles deep inside my chest when I say it. "I'm so sorry, Charlotte." I really am.

So sorry, I could cry. For playing with her emotions;

for leading her on; for getting her into this situation which must be such a big disappointment to her. It's what I wanted to avoid by blowing her off, but I suppose that was naive of me. I couldn't have avoided it, only delayed it. Because she was already too invested in dreams of her own.

It's actually kind of funny, in a morbid way. Both of us travelling here to meet for the same purpose, and still managing to shatter our dreams in the process.

"You know, we could always just be friends," she breaks the silence between us. "I mean, if you'll have me."

"If *I'll* have *you*?" Her words continue to baffle me. How is she putting all this on me? As if I'm the one who's in control? When I'm just a passenger along for a ride, while she holds the reins. I guess I'm learning the meaning of the phrase 'gas lighting' first hand.

"Well, yeah?" she says. "I'm the one inviting myself over here to talk to you, when all you wanted was to be left alone, so…"

"Okay, there's that, but—"

"But at least I managed to say what I came here to say. I'm going to take that as a partial win at least. I wouldn't have had the guts to do it a few years ago. Even if you don't feel the same." She smiles a brief smile and folds her hands and places them in front of herself on the table.

Again, what's with the 'you don't feel the same' nonsense? As if she still stands behind all the bullshit she just told me! How is this all my fault all of a sudden?

Sure, I might have lied by omission which gave her a different view of me than the one present here in the real world, but it's hardly my fault that I don't fit her expectations, is it? I didn't ask her to take things further; the drinks plan was all her idea, which I admittedly should have shot down at the time, but... We shared a nice little fantasy, and now it's over.

"I…I need to go." My head is spinning still. And I still can't get quite enough air, it seems. And I'm getting riled up, which isn't helping any. I need to get out of here, and quickly, before I lose it. I push the table back a little. All the dirty plates and cutlery rattle as a result. People are turning their heads in our direction, then swiftly looking away again. Trying not to gawk at the fat guy struggling to get up.

Charlotte helps me push it further ahead, and a couple of servers rush in to clear the dishes. I can't look them in the eye while I mumble my thanks, because I'm imagining what the plates looked like before. The piles of food I put away, pretending like nobody was watching, when in reality, everyone saw while trying not to stare. Well, everyone except Charlotte. Luckily she only got here once I had already finished.

"Here, I've picked up your things," she says, while gathering the laptop bag containing the pile of notes I'd carried in a misguided attempt to do some last minute prep work during lunch. In the end, there was no prep, only and ungodly amount of food, which I should have foreseen anyway. That's the way things have been going for me for much of this year.

I ought to be ashamed of myself. Hell, I am ashamed. And disgusted. I can't bear to think what people must be telling themselves. How could anyone lets themselves go like that? How dare he make a pig of himself like this in public? He isn't worth the air he breathes.

Worthless. Lazy. Undisciplined. A disgrace.

She waits, holding my bag, while I'm still stuck on my ass. In theory I know what to do. Splay my thighs out wide, lean forward until I can balance on my feet, straighten my knees, and waddle on out of here. But in reality… My knees ache and tremble. My stomach is so stretched tight, I don't know how I'll lean forward without throwing up that last chocolate mousse, or five… My head is fuzzy; what if I get dizzy and fall, taking the table and perhaps Charlotte down with me? The humiliation would be unbearable.

My feet are throbbing and pounding. What if they've fallen asleep and can't take the weight?

Her hand finds its way onto my arm, setting my skin on fire underneath her touch.

"You've got this, Darryl," she says.

If only. If only I could believe a fucking word she says.

Get your fat ugly ass up, you coward! Another voice says; a much more believable voice, which accompanies me every day of my life. *Or are you waiting for them to call a crane to lift your worthless self out of here, making even more of a scene?*

I spread my legs wider until my big belly has just a

little bit more room to sag down and shuffle forward on the bench. My feet start to feel heavier as more weight transfers down onto them. I hold my breath, trying my utmost to counter the tickle in the back of my throat that threatens to call back some of all that food I ate. And I lean ahead, slowly, carefully. God, the pressure on my stomach is intense. Why did I eat so damn much? Why do I not have any self-control when it comes to food? This happened last year as well, though not quite as bad. This happens every time I go anywhere where there's an unlimited buffet. I go completely overboard and regret it once it's too late.

Tears sting in the corners of my eyes as I lean ahead as far as I possibly can and finally, I'm sort of on my feet. For a second, I threaten to fall back into the bench again, but her hand grips my arm more firmly, tugging me forward until I get my balance and straighten my legs.

This is the first time we've met in person. No doubt the last time she ever wants to see my face. And I've needed her help just to get up. I really am a disgrace.

She smiles at me and pats the back of my arm, where she'd just been holding me from. Just my arm is so fat; it must be bigger than her thigh. Disgusting.

For someone who in her own words isn't touchy-feely, she's pretty eager to put her hands on me. It's infuriating, because it makes me feel inconvenient things. Things that I have no business thinking about in this current scenario.

Has she lied about everything? And how the fuck do

I get her to stop before it takes away what's left of my sanity? Until moments ago, I'd worried about having led her on through our messages these past couple of months. Now, the tables have well and truly turned. Her very presence is killing me softly. Another one of those hugs she gave me earlier and I'd actually have a heart attack.

"What's your room number?" she asks.

She isn't seriously planning to follow me to my room, is she? But then again, I couldn't carry that bag if I wanted to, so we're both stuck in this arrangement.

Instead of starting a losing argument, I hand her my keycard and we slowly make our way across the dining hall and towards the lifts in the lobby. One awkward step after another. Every table we pass, we attract stares of shock and horror. With every huff and puff of mine, I die a little more.

I should have never come here. I should have just stayed home, out of sight and out of mind. It wasn't so bad; the same old life I've gotten used to. I was lonely, sure, but the regular comments on my videos offered some respite. And of course her daily emails and messages, which I'm not sure I'm going to be able to live without.

She thanked me earlier, but I should have thanked her instead. Because if it wasn't for her updates and check-ins every day, I might not have been here today. Maybe that's the truth I still owe her. Why she's still lingering around me when it's clear that nothing today is going to go the way she expected. I should do that once we reach my room. Telling my truth might set both of us free, finally.

We make it to the lift, which is already waiting. I'm still thinking of the right words to use, when I am stopped by an inconvenient coughing fit. She rubs and pats my back in an attempt to help. I want to tell her not to trouble herself, but can't. It takes all the energy I have left to suppress that pesky gag reflex, always waiting there in the back of my throat. And then my stomach starts to cramp, right as we exit on my floor, freezing my progress. Once again, I'm covered in sweat, panting and struggling for air. Hello, consequences of my own gluttonous actions.

What could I possibly tell her? What even is the point of it all?

She waits, patiently, rubbing my lower back with her right hand. That's not even where it hurts, and yet it helps, strangely enough.

"Are you okay, Darryl?"

I nod my head, even though that's obviously a lie.

"We're almost there," she tells me, pointing at the door to my room, just a few steps ahead of us.

Good. She can just open the door, dump my bag inside and leave. And then, I'll be able to breathe a little freer. I'll be able to think clearer. I'll be able to drift off and sleep through the aches and pains and terrible reflux that await me. And maybe after that, I'll be able to get through tomorrow's presentation without too much drama, and I'll leave the ruminating and regrets for when I get back home.

"Thanks," I tell her as she touches the keycard to the little pad beside the door, and pushes the door open. "I've got it from here."

I can't quite bring myself to say all the stuff I still owe her. Maybe I'll message her once I can collect my thoughts. I push my way inside and make a very slow, very unsteady beeline for the extra-large bed.

The door clicks shut behind me. This is it, isn't it? I'm never going to see her again. And I never even thanked her properly.

I turn, expecting to see an empty room, but she's still standing there with my laptop bag hanging off her shoulder. What the actual fuck?

She scans the rooms, then her eyes settle on me again and widen just a little bit. She looks lost, and it breaks my heart. Why is she still here? Why would she do this to herself?

"It's okay," I tell her. "Thanks for walking back with me." Jesus Christ, is that really something a grown-ass man needs to be thanking someone for? Apparently I do. I needed that, even if I'd have never willingly admitted it.

Charlotte shakes her head, then her formerly soft gaze turns more resolute. "Oh no. I'm not leaving."

"You're not-- What are you talking about?" I feel so unsteady, I can't put off the inevitable anymore and peel the duvet back before lowering myself onto the bed. It creaks dangerously underneath me, but it holds.

"Look. I heard everything you said down there. And it's okay, really. I'm a big girl and I can handle rejection just fine-_"

"*Rejection* ? What in the world?"

"This is not about that! I refuse to ignore my intuition, especially right now, when it's screaming at me that I'm needed here. It's why I came over even after you cancelled. I cannot bring myself to leave you alone right now."

"This is my room! You can't just stick around when I'm telling you to go!" I argue.

"I'll go once I'm convinced it's right to do so," she says, with a shrug.

I can't deal with this anymore. Although I tried to earlier, I can't even convincingly tell her everything is fine, when it so obviously isn't. She's not fine. I'm not fine. This entire situation is so far from fine, it would be ridiculous to pretend otherwise.

"I'm going to have a nap," I tell her.

"Go for it."

"Right now."

"I'm not stopping you," she says.

She watches with her arms crossed in front of her as I try to shimmy back onto the squishy bed and lie down on my side. I try not to think about how fucking embarrassing this whole situation is, but hey, I've seemingly hit new lows today already, so what does it matter?

Now, trapped on my side, I try to kick my shoes off, which fails miserably, so I just try to keep my feet hanging just off the edge of the bed. Then I feel around for the duvet, which is partially trapped underneath me, so I can't even cover myself properly. Then I realise that the lights are still on, and the curtains are open. And I still can't breathe properly even though lying on my side is usually the only position that works for me. I guess if I keep going like this, soon I'll have to start sleeping while sitting upright, like some of those people you see on *My 600lb Life* .

Fucking pathetic. I'm not nearly that big yet. Or am I? I stopped weighing myself once I maxed out my scale at just under 400lbs a few months back. Since then, I might have added a little more, but it can't be that much.

Every breath hurts my chest. Every attempt to get at the duvet leaves me more frustrated.

Charlotte sighs audibly as she walks back to the door and switches off the lights, and then makes her way to the other side of the bed, somewhere behind me, and I hear the curtains being drawn. As if she could read my mind.

Now, in the half-dark, I start to calm down just a little. Just enough to be able to breathe a little deeper.

But then, she's at my feet, and I tense up again as she gets my shoes off.

"Thanks," I grumble.

God, that feels so much better, though. If I wasn't also so ashamed.

And then, moments later, she's behind me on the bed, tugging the edge of the duvet out from underneath me until it's free, and she is able to drape it over me, tucking me in. And that's when I feel the first tears streaming down my face. Luckily they're silent tears. And it's pretty dark, because I really can't have her see me like this.

There's a bit of rustling and movement on the mattress behind me, and I feel a warmth against my back, and her hand, resting on my hair.

"I'm sorry for being so pushy. Especially since you've made it very clear you don't want me here. I just get this sense, that you shouldn't be alone right now."

Suddenly, the next lot of tears aren't so silent anymore. Who said I didn't want her here? I mean, I kind of insinuated it, but I didn't mean it; not really.

"I wouldn't be here if not for you," I say. Her hand pauses for a moment, then starts to caress my hair in long, relaxing strokes. "Over this past year, I had so many mornings where I didn't feel a reason to get out of bed. Until your emails started coming."

"I've had plenty of mornings like that too. Until I found your channel."

I shake my head. She's not getting me. "No, really. Thank *you*. "

"Darryl. It's okay, really."

Her fingernails scratch ever so deliciously against my scalp as she continues to caress me. It's so intoxicating I can't bring myself to tell her to stop. Even though she should. She ought to stop and leave like I asked her to earlier.

"I cancelled, because this is what I was afraid of," I say. "I never wanted you to see this. I didn't want your pity."

"Pity?" She shifts closer to me and caresses my face with the back of her hand. I'm still weeping, and as such, tears stain the both of us. "I don't pity you."

"No? Then what's all this?"

"It's empathy. Because I'd like to think I know a little bit about how you feel."

I let out a scoff. "How could you? You're... You're magnificent. And I'm a terrible failure of a human being."

She leans across me and presses her face against mine, taking a deep breath. "How can that be, when you've completely changed my life? I have been unable to write for years; I felt so paralysed every time I sat down to try. It got me questioning everything; my whole identity, in fact. To lose the one thing you've always dreamed of doing; it's a deep and hopeless sort of a pain..."

I shut my eyes and just lay there, trying not to think too much about her gorgeous body, pressed up against my back, and her elegant hand cupping my face as she continues to cuddle with me. It's sweet torture, having her so close to me. So warm. So sticky.

After everything she told me about herself; in the various communications we've shared, I never expected anything like this. I never imagined that she'd be this assertive. That after the complete shit show of our first meeting; we'd end up in this position.

Pity is the only logical answer for it. She doesn't know the depths of my depravity; or she'd never put herself in my room. In my bed.

If I wasn't so absolutely stuffed and useless, she'd push me to do things I'd never even consider in the real world. I'd have a thick, throbbing erection, ready to enter her right this moment. I don't know if I'd be able to control that urge. If I'd-- *Shit.*

Obviously she has no idea about any of it. She would have run by now.

"And with the help of your videos, I got my voice back, Darryl. I actually finished a book yesterday. It was going to be a surprise. In case you wanted to read it, that is. I know how busy you must be."

"That's wonderful, Charlotte. I'm happy for you." My voice cracks as I speak. I am pleased, but also conflicted. Because I wish I could say the same. I wish I could write something new too, but I've been hopelessly stuck ever since...

Ever since last year.

"But that's all on you, though," I tell her. "It's your achievement. Not mine."

She tightens her grip around me, now no longer holding my face, but hugging me around the upper part of my torso. Our size difference makes it quite comical. But then, why do I still feel like crying rather than laughing?

"I was getting nowhere on my own. It's the effect you've had on me. You inspired me. You got me to believe in myself again. I actually started it just before sending you that first email. I poured all of myself into those pages. It's the best thing I've ever written, I think."

I put my hand on her arm; no longer content to lie there, limply and lifelessly, without reciprocating her affections. She feels so small under my touch, yet so strong.

She sighs, her breath tickling the side of my face, and hugs me tighter.

"I know I can get a bit intense. A bit crazy..." she whispers. "It's been a failing of mine, which I've tried to work on, but... Well, I've always been sensitive. I've always had a tendency to fall fast and hard. Like I've fallen for you. So I took all that and committed it to the page. I couldn't have done it without you, inspiring me."

Her words make me tense up again. And my inner cynic is back for another fight.

"Don't. Please don't," I protest, once again feeling the shame of fresh tears. "I know what you're trying to do, and it's not going to work."

"What am I trying to do?" she asks. She's got the innocent routine down pat. I've got to give her that.

"You're telling me what you think I want to hear. You're playing a game. I don't know how you do it, but right from the start in every email and every message, you always figure out just what it is I want to hear and then you... How do you always know?" I'm getting more and more worked up, and raise my voice at her. Which makes me even more ashamed of myself. So what if she's trying to be kind to me right now? Because deep down I know I *do* need it.

"Oh, but I'm just trying to tell you the truth. It's not a game to me." She's still hanging onto me. How glad I am for that, because to lose her affection now would rip my heart straight out of my chest.

"I've done nothing for you. I've been selfish, wishing and hoping that your emails would never stop coming-- Of course now they will, but I can't bear to think of that just yet."

"I know it sounds crazy, but I'll never stop," she says. "I'll never give up hope. I know that this right here is temporary. I know that once this moment passes, and you don't feel so vulnerable anymore, you'll ask me to leave and that will be that. And I'll still love you even then. No matter where we both are."

Her words continue to shake me to my core. Does she have any idea how insane any of this sounds? How obsessive...

"You have no idea what you're talking about. You don't. You can't possibly mean any of this," I protest.

"I know enough," she says.

It takes every ounce of my strength to free myself from her grasp and heave and shove my overgrown body onto my back and then onto my other side to face her properly. Sweat is dripping from my brow and my heart hammering away in my throat, when I've finally made it.

Despite the half-dark that surrounds us I can see her look down at me, with tears in her eyes too. But also with a strange kind of strength and resolve emanating from her gaze. Like a willful teenager, but without the explosive temper and irrationality. Like she knows exactly who she is and what she wants. Even if she couldn't possibly. Because nobody I know has ever been that single-minded about anything.

Plus, everything she believes is based on a lie. It's how I've presented myself to the world for years. It's the image I've portrayed, of someone who's worth something. The truth, however, should put a stop to all this craziness.

"I'm worth shit. I'm a fake, don't you see? I don't know a damn thing about what I've been talking about. I've been parroting advice heard from other sources. I haven't had an original thought in... Well probably forever."

She shakes her head. "I've read all your work. Including those short stories you published on your blog all those years ago. You're immensely talented."

"I wrote a cheap *Lord of the Rings* copy. It has all been done before; said before. There's nothing original or new in any of it. No wonder I haven't been able to do more. I've run out of things to steal."

For the briefest of moments, a smile appears on her lips, which infuriates me further.

"I'm worthless. A loser. Good for nothing. I have nothing to contribute to the world, don't you see? I keep making videos about stuff others have already talked about, in the hopes that sooner or later I have some kind of epiphany or breakthrough and I might actually have something to add. But there's nothing there. I'm a failure."

"Darryl..." the way she whispers my name gives me goosebumps. And the way she looks at me when she says it will make me cry all over again, so I avoid her gaze. Jesus, isn't this enough humiliation for one day?

"I'm a failure," I say again.

"Darryl, tell me..." She rests her hand on my cheek again, almost forcing me to look up at her.

"What?"

"Whose words are these, Darryl? Because they're not yours," she says. Her expression is so serious now, almost making me doubt that I ever even saw a smile on her face only a few seconds ago.

"Whose...?"

"Who said these things to you? Who tried to tear you down like this?" she asks again, while running her fingers through my hair, sweetly; patiently.

I shut my eyes because I can't stand the way her eyes seem to pierce my subconscious. All those lectures. All those rants. Sometimes without the belt, but mostly with. And ever since he passed, I've been hearing his voice every day, ringing in my ears so loud I couldn't hear my own thoughts anymore.

"My father."

"He was wrong, though," she says.

I shake my head. No, because I've proven him right every single day. I literally proved him right every time I went back to the buffet earlier.

"Lazy, greedy, good for nothing..."

"No, Darryl."

I open my eyes again, only to see her shaking her head at me.

"There are thousands of people out there, waiting for

you to speak to them during your presentation tomorrow. Just like I did, Darryl. Because you understand the things that stand in our way. You understand, more than anyone."

"But I don't, though." I complain. "I couldn't even make it to this room without your help. I'm a disgrace of a human being."

"We couldn't do what we do without a few demons in the closet, Darryl. None of us. We write to deal with what haunts us in our darkest moments. You taught me to accept that, and once I really understood what it meant, everything started to fall into place and the words came back."

"How will I face them after what happened at the buffet? You didn't see. You couldn't possibly understand."

"I saw everything."

"You did?" I stammer.

"I'm so sorry; I'd been spying on you for about an hour. Until I finally had the guts to come up to you." Her expression twists with sadness, no, with shame, as she speaks. It's such a familiar emotion to me; it's hard to miss now that I'm actually looking at her again.

"Shit, you were watching..." I'm almost speechless, except for one question that I just can't shake. "Then why didn't you run?"

"Don't you understand? I've admired your work from afar for so long. Your books as well as your teachings. But it's really the darkness in you that attracts me. It is what fuels the depths of my obsession," her voice is flat and low as she speaks. "I've seen glimpses of it in your videos, but now... I could feel it right across the hall, as though you were calling out to me."

Her words send goosebumps down my back. I can't say for sure that she isn't putting on an act, but I'm starting to doubt my earlier observations now. Maybe she's been telling the truth all along. How the hell would I know? I've never been in this position. I've had fan mail about my books, but never anything like *this*. It's powerful; scary almost. Or, it would be scary if she wasn't also so fucking kind and caring to me.

Still, she doesn't *really* know. She's been falling for an illusion. And no matter how I wish I could hide or ignore it, I have to tell her.

"It wasn't just today. This has been my life. I know I should stop, but I can't. And it's been getting worse and worse. I must have gained at least 100lb over the past year, ever since..."

"Since your father passed," she says, while reaching over and squeezing my hand.

Her words sting me right into my core. How can she know these things which I myself am just barely starting to put together just now. I've been proving him right in all of my actions. I've been on a collision course with an inevitable destiny which he laid out for me with his endless criticisms and harsh judgements.

"Yeah."

"I know," she adds.

"How?"

She shrugs and smiles briefly again. "Intuition, I

guess? Plus, I've been watching your content rather closely."

"And you're still here?"

"I'm not going anywhere." It sounds outlandish, but I'm starting to believe her.

"Why?"

"Because I love you. You helped me find my purpose again. I owe you everything I have."

"But... that's indebtedness; it's duty. That's not love." And it makes her sound like a stalker. Or a codependent. I'm not sure which is worse.

"Oh, but I'm certain that it is." She smiles briefly, and my shock and confusion lifts a little.

"But real, actual love requires an element of physical attraction, and you couldn't possibly--" I argue.

"I could and I am."

"Attracted to *me* ?!" I wonder aloud. She couldn't be!

"Never felt it more strongly in my life. I'm finding you quite impossible to resist, actually," she whispers.

Her eyes are fixated on me. On mine. On my lips, and occasionally, glancing down lower at my body. A body which I wish I could hide away.

"I'm nothing. No one."

She places her index finger on my lips. "Not your words. And certainly not mine. To me, you're everything."

I shake my head. "No. You are. You're magnificent. The most beautiful woman I've ever laid eyes on." A bit of a crazy stalker, but hey, nobody's perfect. Plus, if I'm entirely honest with myself, I've been swept up by obsession as well when it comes to her. Refreshing my inbox every five seconds, waiting for her daily emails to come. I can hardly judge her for something I've been struggling with too.

She shyly glances away when I reach up and push a few strands of errand hair out of her face. Now that my eyes have adjusted to the dim lighting, I see she's blushing and I can't stop staring at her pretty face and her flush red lips.

Despite everything; the awkwardness of these moments shared with her; the very intense physical discomfort I'm still in after my overindulgences at the buffet... Despite everything, I realize I actually *have* been fucking hard throughout our interactions so far. In fact, my cock, straining against the confines of my jeans is a large part of the discomfort I currently feel. I just hadn't realised it fully until this moment.

I have a stalker. A devotee. *Me!* Maybe this should worry me, but mainly it continues to baffle me instead.

"You can't want this. Can't want me," I mumble, mostly to myself, while visualising how I must look underneath the duvet, weirdly posed on my side, with all the rolls and dips and folds my overgrown body tends to make in this position. I can't quite imagine it, which is probably for the best.

"Why? Because you're fat?" she asks.

Again, her candidness shocks me into silence. Because, yes, that's exactly what I was getting at, but I chose to dance around the issue.

"Respectfully." She licks her lips while staring down

at me. "So fucking what? Gives me more to love."

God. That's about all I can take. My hand reaches down at my crotch, almost with a mind of its own. I'm throbbing and aching down there; hopelessly trapped by the waistband that's been cutting deep into my flesh ever since I ate so damn much. I can't even get at it properly, plus any stimulation at all is going to end this moment much too soon.

She rolls away, off her side of the bed, flips the duvet open and slips under the covers beside me. Her warm body presses into mine, and her eager little hands find mine and get to work on my belt, which is cutting me, deeply.

It'll be a relief to get it off, and also... My earlier shame is creeping up on me again. With a firm tug and some wiggling on her part, she's able to open the buckle, and I'm released as the button of my jeans pops off, my zip opens and the excesses of lunch are able to make their escape at last. It's like one of those croissant-dough-in-a-can type situations, where when the seal is broken, all of the mass contained within just suddenly expands and spills out. Surely this is the moment she regrets her earlier words and pulls away! Surely, this is the final straw.

She doesn't. She caresses my belly, ever so gently, while I can barely even look her in the eye.

She wants me. Claims to *love* me. Who the fuck am I to refuse?

"Close your eyes," she whispers, while leaning in to kiss my face. Her lips are soft, her breath like a whisper against my cheeks, my forehead, finally, against my eyelids.

I do as I'm told and I slip into a deeper, calmer sort of darkness, just as her hands find my shoulders, and one of her arms slips in underneath my neck, pulling her against me again.

"Close your eyes and feel me."

"But..." I'm unable to speak much through ragged breaths. Now no longer gasping for air because of being overstuffed, but rather, because she's overwhelmed me.

"Darryl, you're fucking gorgeous. Try to feel what I feel."

That doesn't make a whole lot of sense to me, but I try to focus anyway. Her hand rests on my chest for a moment as I inhale, and so does she, then exhales against my lips. It tickles, and yet I wouldn't dare change a thing about it. Her lips are so close, I can sense them, but I keep my eyes shut as instructed, and just try to imagine what she might look like right now.

Her body, under the covers with me, the pointy tips of her full breasts pressed against my torso like little darts. The gentle curve of her lower abdomen brushing past my belly with every breath. Her hand, warm and determined, as it travels downward and slips underneath my t-shirt, peeling it over my huge bloated body, which dips heavily into the soft mattress between us.

She runs her fingertips across my bare skin. On my side, up and down the folds and rolls of excess flesh, then buries her face into the side of my neck; kissing, nibbling, suckling.

I groan, loudly, so desperate am I for more of her touch. More where it matters.

I've never been very fond of appetizers; I always prefer to get to the main course or better yet, skip ahead to dessert...

But she, like most women perhaps, seeming likes to stretch things out. I am grateful, because if she so much as touched my cock, it'd be game over for me. And then... Well, surely, this is going to be one time deal, especially if I disappoint her.

"Can you feel my heartbeat?" she asks, as she takes my hand and places it onto her cleavage. I don't know about *that* , but I can feel other things...

The heat coming off her; the softness of her skin which could make me weep all over again... I can even feel as all the little hairs on her body stand upright to attention. And her breaths quicken underneath my touch and caress my neck.

I can feel her pull away ever so slightly; not enough to startle me, but enough to make me anticipate her next move. With a soft gasp, she lets our lips touch for the very first time.

I moan into her mouth. Loudly, desperately.

"You are gorgeous," she tells me again. "Your body pleases me."

It's a funny thing to tell someone, and yet it's once again exactly what I needed to hear. She silences further, even louder moans with her tongue, which slips in between my lips and starts dancing around mine, coaxing it into a tango the likes of which I've never experienced.

Actually, I've never experienced anything like this moment. Previous experiences with other women were always initiated by me. Always in a rush. Always a bit ashamed and apologetic, and designed to be over quickly, as to not inconvenience them much.

Because no woman could possibly want me like this. No woman could possibly desire me or my inadequate body... Except her. She's been pursuing me relentlessly for the past four months. With her emails and her little teases and suggestive jokes. She's been reeling me in. Resistance is futile. Plus, I've never been pursued. Why would I ever want to resist this? It's the most exciting thing ever to have happened to me. If she turns out to be a psycho and turns on me afterwards, praying mantis style, I'll go with a big smile on my face.

"I want you. Fuck, I want you so bad," she whines.

"I want you," I tell her. "I love you."

She smiles into my lips. Mind, I've still got my eyes closed, so I notice it by touch alone. And she wraps her other arm around my neck as well, hugging me tightly against her.

For a moment, I'm lost; both hands on her toned back as she writhes into me. Then, in a sudden rush of confidence, I reach down and grab a handful of firm ass, dragging her hips against me.

She squeals and bucks her hips in my direction, which encourages me further.

I roll onto my back, taking her with me. She rewards me with her hands, grabbing at my full man tits; both at once, and tweaking my nipples just hard enough to send jolts of pleasure through me.

I didn't know I could feel like this. I didn't know...

"I love you!" she whispers, in between further kisses. Across my lips, my cheeks, my neck. It's nice to be enveloped by the dark like this. To just *feel* it. Because that way I can convince myself that I'm allowed to enjoy it. I'm able to pretend like she enjoys it too.

I guess that's why she told me to shut my eyes. How did she know?

Charlotte:

When I open my eyes, I have the perfect vantage point on top of him. I see his face, flush with excitement and damp with sweat, but also more at ease than I've seen it ever since I first laid eyes on him.

Even more at ease than in his earlier videos; the ones he published long before I ever knew his name. When he was about 100lbs lighter by his own admission. Not that I care about that specifically. I only care about what it represents. I care about the struggle he's been going through all alone. I never knew the depths of it except for the little hints peppered through his emails, newsletters and blog posts, which neither of us ever elaborated on.

Still, I was right in my interpretations. I was correct in what I saw.

All along, I've seen a man who has some depth to him. Some substance. The only man who could ever move me like this. Who inspired me like no other. Who was screaming out for someone to understand.

I didn't know at the time, but I always saw it. And that's why I fell.

And now I'm lying on top of him; I might as well be on top of the world. The pudgy little part of my lower abdomen rests on his rather substantial belly. On top of all those platefuls of food he stuffed into himself down in the dining hall.

I had watched in horror at what he was doing, because I didn't understand. But now... I'm turned on by what it's done to his body. It's so hard underneath me. So full. So ripe. So ready to burst.

Much like his cock, which is sticking up through the softness of his full thighs. He's barely a couple of pumps away from release; I know it. And yet, something tells me that his first release will only be the first of many. Certainly, if I've got something to say about it, we'll not get out of bed for hours to come. Because the next few hours are for cumming. For both of us.

His arms hold me firmly in place on top of him. His big, squishy arms. God, they're huge. He's huge. He dwarfs me and I love it.

I've never known the pleasures a man of his size could dole out. Every part of him is built to please me. He *is* gorgeous, though he probably won't know no matter how many times I try to tell him.

Words mean nothing in these situations. Actions are everything.

"Unzip me," I tell him, guiding his hand to my side. He frowns through closed eyes as he fumbles with the tab of the zip until finally it gives way. I sit up, wiggling from side to side to get it off the top of my hips and up and over my head. Within a split second, I've unclasped my bra also, and thrown it off the side of the bed.

Men are visual creatures. Seeing me might give him more pleasure than exploring me by touch. But I don't tell him to open his eyes yet. His shame about his own appearance appears so deep; it seems to be helping him a lot to do this completely blind.

But, selfishly, I do not close *my* eyes again. I admire him. His full lips. The way his vast chest rises and falls with every urgent breath. The way his much larger hands look cupping my breasts.

I stare down at the contrast between my petite waist and his large round belly which sits proudly between us. And the little trail of hair that's visible just below the bottom hem of his t-shirt. Should I risk it? Can I get rid of it? I want nothing more than to see what's hidden underneath, which I've so far only explored with stolen caresses and my rather over active imagination.

I lean back, letting my buttocks crush down against his erection. He shudders and lets out a ragged moan through moist, parted lips. So beautiful. So perfect. While he's distracted, I start ridding him of the t-shirt. But it's stuck. He's still preoccupied, massaging my boob with one hand, and digging his other into my naked thigh in an attempt to rub himself to ecstasy against my arse.

So long as we're both being selfish... I claw at the t-shirt, and once my fingernail makes a small tear in it, I yank it apart until it splits with a satisfying noise. And there, I have my reward. Just the right amount of chest hair, which I'm compelled to pet immediately; up and down, from just below the neckline of the t-shirt all the way down the rather long and mountainous happy trail.

I can't suppress a gasp, showing my appreciation.

Our eyes meet for a moment. So worried still; I guess I have a bit more convincing to do before we re on the on the same page. But as soon as I rub my palms against his tits again and grind my ass down into his cock, he relaxes again and his lids shut. Or his lids shut and then he relaxes again; I'm not sure which comes first.

He knows. He knows and he likes it like this. Maybe with his eyes closed, he pretends like I'm not really looking either. But I wouldn't miss this sight for the world. There is perfection in the contrast between us. Everything he would consider a flaw, I appreciate it enough for the both of us.

I lean down against his hot naked chest and take his nipple in between my lips, flicking my tongue across it a few times. He's moaning again. I love how loud he is. How raw and uninhibited. It gives me the confidence to reciprocate and tell him in animalistic grunts and groans just how horny I am for him.

While leant forward, I lift off his crotch for a moment and try to get at his cock, which had so far still been obscured underneath his boxers. He helps me with his right hand, but not without grabbing a fistful and giving it a good pump, eliciting more moans and shudders that creep across the vastness of his big body.

I never knew how hot sex with a fat guy could be. Never thought about it until him. Jesus, I've been missing out! I've literally never been this involved; this wet; this horny. Sex has always been a bit of a chore for me with previous boyfriends. Something that you're supposed to do every so often, but which I never wanted for just for myself.

I've always found solo activities much easier and more satisfying...I've never even initiated a sexual encounter in my life. Until just now. Until Darryl.

It's what he inspired me to write about. A beautifully passionate love affair that makes up the central part of the plot of the novel I dedicated to him. Finally, after wasting so much time and even more of my mental peace, I discovered the kind of writer I was always meant to be.

Not of crime and fantasy and horror and who knows what else, but of erotic fiction. I was built to write provocative romance; to really dig down into what makes people tick and more importantly, what makes them *feel.*

He did that for me. That is my purpose. And not just to commit it to paper, but to show it to him firsthand. It occurs to me that although I meant to simply *confess* my feelings to him today, I actually wanted *this.* I wanted to show him. I wanted for him to feel what I feel.

Every last gasp, groan and shudder of it.

And judging by his reaction as I finally lower myself down onto the tip of his erect cock, I've succeeded. He trembles all over as he holds his breath for a second.

Then he moans again. A most beautiful sound which I've never heard before today. Vulnerable and joyful and painful all at once.

It's more like a howl than those sanitised, fake moans you hear during porn or sex scenes on TV. There's nothing posed or stilted about this moment. The moment when his thick, quivering cock enters me and stretches my cunt to its limits. So long has it been. So long have I waited to feel this way.

"Oh god," I cry out. "Oh fucking hell!"

I rest both my hands against his belly and start to move. Slowly up and down. It takes me a minute to find my rhythm, and more importantly, to figure out how much I can move without him slipping out of me. His great big thighs and lower part of his belly try to compete and get in the way, but with some persistence and help from both his hands grasping me firmly by my thighs, I find the right angle and the right speed.

He's not a talker, just a moaner. His face is wet now, with sweat as well as what look like a few errand tears. I don't mind it; don't mind the supposed negative emotions he's been expressing so freely in front of me. It's how I know he's being real. A *real* man. Not a pretend manly-man who only shows his feelings when speaking of his favourite football team.

My cunt is sopping wet and my lower abdomen feels tight enough to bounce a penny off of. I'm so close; have been ever since we started cuddling... And I know by the deep furrow in his brow that he's fighting his release with every move of mine. Fighting the inevitable, which will set both of us free. If it's permission he wants, he has it as far as I'm concerned.

"Cum for me, baby," I whisper, before giving him a good few pumps, tightening myself as I go. Those Kegels I've been doing are paying off now.

His moans quicken as his breaths shallow. "Charlotte, fuck!"

"Go on. I need to feel you fill me up with your cum!" I ride him faster; harder. My thighs burn; so tight am I forced to stretch to accommodate his large hips between me. But it's a good sort of pain. The kind that reminds you that you're doing something worthwhile.

I'm about to cry out more encouragements, when he goes rigid and his fingers dig into my thigh rather harshly. The pain is enough to tip me over the edge, along with the shudder of his dick spurting hot seed into the deepest part of my vagina.

I flop down on top of him, wrapping my arms around his neck again just as he hugs me tight.

"You're... Fucking... Amazing," he tells me.

I can't get enough of him. Of his lips, which I kiss again and again; his hands on my back. His chest rising and falling rapidly with quick shallow gasps for air. The way his bottom lip feels when I suck on it and run my tongue across it.

It's all so perfect. So beautiful. I'm home.

"You're amazing. The best," I say.

He doesn't say anything, just holds me tighter. My face ends up in the crook of his neck, which I love as well. So soft is the skin there, how it wrinkles there where his shoulders and neck join, all of him is so soft; so tactile. So fucking sexy.

As our breaths slow a little, his grip on me loosens, as if he's slipping away. I can barely feel his cock inside me anymore. Is this how the moment passes? Is our dream over already?

I move a little to the left and grab his big, saggy man boob with my right hand. As if to tell him that it's still on. I'm still here and ready. He trembles a little when I start nibbling on his neck.

He clears his throat; his big firm belly jerking upwards into me while he does so. "I'm sorry." His voice still sounds choked.

I shake my head. "No."

"I know I couldn't possibly live up to--"

"Nope!" He flinches at the firmness of my tone. "You don't get to apologise after giving me the best fuck of my life." I lean up and meet his gaze.

He's quiet again.

I grab his chubby face and press my lips against his while giving him a good dose of tongue. He groans into my mouth and I feel something stir there at the entrance of my pussy. My message is getting across.

I pull back just far enough to look him in the eye again. "Best fuck of my life so far."

"That's..." I grind my hips down, making him moan again before being able to finish his sentence. "That's what I'm supposed to say."

That makes me smile. "Great. Then let's do it again." His eyes flag for a moment at my suggestion.

His hair is sticky with sweat, and his face still flush. And he hasn't yet caught his breath even though I'm quite calm by now. I like him even better looking destroyed like this. Maybe that's why I started getting all warm in my chest when I had to help him up off his seat earlier. And why I couldn't resist touching him once he clumsily got into bed. Because the exhausted state he was in reminded me of what this moment would look like. Yes, that makes sense. I was imagining his post-orgasmic exhaustion face...

"Again," he gasps.

Oh, I love how eager he is. Like he'll be unable to resist me, no matter how tired he gets. I wonder how many times I'll be able to push my luck with him in a single day or night. Maybe if I tease him first...

I climb off, eliciting a loudly moaned 'no' from him as his semi slips out of me and flops heavily onto his thigh. Beautifully decadent. Just like the rest of him. His protests stop once I close my fist around his length and feel it growing under my touch.

God yes. Perfection.

I kneel down beside him and a couple of quick pumps later, I bring the tip of his cock to my lips. It tastes of me; salty sweet but nice. I don't mind it; I've tasted it before.

From down here, I can't see; his belly is just too big for us to look past. That's too bad, since I imagine he would love the view of me sucking him off. How I purse my lips to fit around his growing length. How I run the tip of my tongue across the bulbous head of his cock. How my cheeks fill when I get as much of him as possible in there and give it a good suck.

His breaths have turned to gasps and non-stop moans again. His hand is in my hair, guiding me into a rhythm he likes without ever being forceful. So perfect. Unlike the last guy I did this with.

If he hasn't got the message so far, of how much I love and value him. I hope he's getting it now. His hand in my hair grows twitchier, telling me he's getting closer again. And I am anyway still slick and ready... Should I let him cum in my mouth? Or do I push for another release of my own?

I'm bobbing up and down his cock, fondling his balls which are almost fully obscured in the deep squishy fat of his inner thighs while I try to decide. Until he nudges at my head.

"Baby, stop," he gasps.

That's the first time he's called me baby. I lovingly run my tongue across the ridges surrounding the head of his cock.

"Stop, please."

I'm in half a mind to keep going, but I pull away, leaning on his thigh and raise my head high enough to see across his belly and chest. His eyebrows are pulled together, his lips parted and moist. He's so obviously gagging for it. Why won't he let me finish him off again? It would be so easy, so satisfying.

"I don't know if--" he begins.

"I want to make you feel good," I explain.

He pauses and stares at my lips. Perhaps he has been

imagining the sight of me sucking him dry... Maybe next time he could watch my reflection in a mirror, or something.

"I want to try it, you know, the old fashioned way." He glances away from me, and down at himself. "Though I don't know if I'll be able..."

Him on top? What a glorious idea. I could touch him all over; feel his mighty big body on top of me...

"I don't want to hurt you," he tells me.

"You won't!" I sit down beside him and watch patiently as he slowly but surely gets onto his knees. His big belly is sagging down quite low, but with a bit of adjustment, this should be possible.

I lie down against the pillows and spread wide while he positions himself. He looks so tired, bless him. And a bit scared. It melts my heart and makes me even wetter, all at once.

Once he's in between my legs and I'm spread as wide as can be, I try to work out the logistics. His belly would need shifting a little, up on top of me. I try to get my hand in underneath to reach for his cock. It's quite far away.

His eyes evade me, and his face falls. He's close to giving up, but I won't accept that. I will not have any part of this experience be a disappointment. It's my purpose to make him feel good, not inadequate, and I'm determined to follow through.

"If you kneel, and get my hips part of the way onto your thighs?" I suggest.

Sweat drips from his forehead onto my tummy. I

reach for his face and wait for his eyes to meet mine finally. "I can't wait to feel you inside me again."

That seems to help. He takes deep breath and pulls me up into the fold underneath his belly, onto his thighs and sure enough, I can feel the tip of his swollen cock press up against me. The angle is almost right.

I shift his belly up just a little until it rests heavily on top of me. "Push, baby," I tell him.

He goes down onto his elbows on top of me, and with a bit of pushing and wiggling, he slips inside of me. All the while his immense weight rests mostly on top of me. I can hardly catch my breath, but it's glorious.

"Oh fuck yes!" I whisper. He starts to push in and out, slowly. He's dripping with sweat all over now. But the best part is that he's actually looking at me now. And in his eyes, I can see so much which was previously hidden. His worries; his doubts; his fears. They're all on display. I wrap my arms around his neck, barely, because he's just so big, making it hard to reach.

"Shit, you're so good," I tell him. "This feels so good!"

With every push, he calms a little. With every thrust, a little more of his doubts seem to fade.

Every time he buries his cock into me as far as it'll go, he takes my breath away with his sheer size. And the moans... The moans are even more glorious like this. Breathless, shameless, beautiful sounds of pleasure.

"Fuck me hard, Darryl," I tell him.

He speeds up. Between him, his immense heft, and the squishiness of the mattress below, I'm swept up in the moment. It feels like being stuck in a powerful current; where outside forces decide how and when you move, and you yourself no longer hold any power. It's breathtaking; a total loss of control.

I couldn't move if I wanted to. I can't even breathe unless he lets me. All I can do is kiss him, caress him, grab and fondle him. I can barely hug him, but I try. In the end I decide to just put one hand on the side of his face, and the other on his tit, between us. And lost for words or breath, I can hardly do anything beyond looking into his beautiful eyes and moaning his name. Similarly, he stares back, right into my soul, and moans those same beautiful moans of his.

Raw ones. Unedited and uncensored ones. Even in my wildest dreams, I couldn't have foreseen the sounds he's making now. And I'm glad. Because although I've fantasised about this moment so many times; hell, I wrote a whole book about it even, I'm grateful for the entirely new experiences he's giving me.

He's turning redder as he carries on. His eyes are betraying how close he is to his limits. How spent and how tired, and yet fighting for another release. Or is he fighting to hold back long enough to give me one? I can't yet tell, until the truth reveals itself.

By the clenching of my entire lower abdomen, squeezing and pulsating around his thick cock. By the uncontrollable scream of pleasure that passes through my lips. By the way my fingernails dig into his upper arm, piercing skin along the way.

By the way I cry out his name, as he buries himself

deeply into my cunt and stays there, weighing my body down heavily underneath his big bulk.

Until he starts to twitch and tremble as well, and I feel a second load of hot cum deposited into my vagina, filling me with a heat that only seeks to heighten my orgasm, which seems to last an eternity of a few seconds, during which all goes black and I no longer know anything, except his embrace. And the shudder of his belly on top of me, as he fights for air, while I myself can get none.

Until he leans up on his elbows, allowing me to fill my lungs again.

And I realize I'm crying. Tears of joy, running down my smiling face. And he leans in to kiss me. Salty, beautiful kisses, underlining just how perfect this moment is. How for once in my life, I wasn't wrong. My instincts were spot on.

It was his purpose to put his wisdom out into the world, even if he continues to underestimate himself; haunted by voices of the past. And it was mine to receive his message; to reach out to him and love him until he'd finally understand. We may have some way to go before he does. Before some of his darkness lifts off, allowing him to clearly see the truth I already know.

We are perfectly meant to be. Everything right now-- from my arms around his neck and his cock deeply buried inside of me--is exactly how it should be. I am his. He is mine. And I'm never letting go. Because whatever he does next, I'm always going to be his biggest fan. And I love him more than I love myself.

ABOUT THE AUTHOR

Dear Reader,

If you came across me in real life, you'd never guess the kind of filth I like to read and write. Cleverly disguised as a boring office worker, the drudgery of my 9-to-5 only becomes bearable because of my vivid and explicit imagination. I like fat guys and I cannot lie. In my world, bigger (fatter) is always better. It's been that way for as long as I can remember.

Thanks for reading this story, one of hopefully many of my published sexual fantasies. My stories revolve around one common theme: really big men and the women who can't help but lust for them.

Although I like porn just fine, it's nearly impossible to find it in the flavour that I desire. The written word allows me to explore a world of lush excess that mainstream adult entertainment just cannot provide. When I started writing, I soon discovered the beauty of having a catalog of erotica out there to satisfy my own lustful needs. This is a passion project more than a money-grab.

So, first and foremost, my writing is for me. But perhaps there are other women (or even men) out there who share my tastes; my fetishes and fantasies? My fascination with the larger male form, and sexualisation of food (especially overeating). If that sounds like something you'll wank off to, you've come to the right place.

xxx Hedonist

To find out more, check:

❖ eXplicitTales.com

www.ingramcontent.com/pod-product-compliance
Lightning Source LLC
Chambersburg PA
CBHW070512170726

48291CB00008B/2719